Two Little Monkeys

MEM FOX · JILL BARTON

Beach Lane Books · New York London Toronto Sydney New Delhi

Two little monkeys
playing near a tree,
one named Cheeky,
one named Chee.

Hello, Cheeky!
Hello, Chee!
Better stay close
to that big old tree!

Look out, Cheeky!
Look out, Chee!
Something's prowling—
what could it be?

Two little monkeys
run to a tree,
one named Cheeky,
one named Chee.

Scramble up, Cheeky!
Scramble up, Chee!
Scramble up
that big old tree!

Two little monkeys
tremble in a tree,
one named Cheeky,
one named Chee.

Hide away, Cheeky!
Hide away, Chee!
Make sure you're hidden
in that big old tree!

Two little monkeys
peep from a tree,
one named Cheeky,
one named Chee.

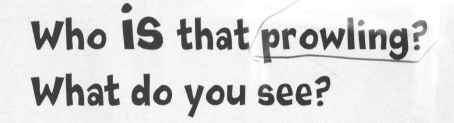

Who **is** that prowling?
What do you see?

Careful, Cheeky!
Careful, Chee!
Don't fall out
of that big old tree!

Two little monkeys **leap** from a tree!
One named Cheeky,
one named Chee.

Well done, Cheeky!
Well done, Chee!
What a brave leap
from that big old tree!

And now you're safe—

as safe can be.

You clever little monkeys,
Cheeky and Chee!

For Cate, with love

—M. F.

For Nat, Soph, and Al, Livi and H.

—J. B.

BEACH LANE BOOKS
An imprint of Simon & Schuster Children's Publishing Division
1230 Avenue of the Americas, New York, New York 10020
Text copyright © 2012 by Mem Fox
Illustrations copyright © 2012 by Jill Barton
BEACH LANE BOOKS is a trademark of Simon & Schuster, Inc.
For information about special discounts for bulk purchases, please contact Simon & Schuster Special Sales
at 1-866-506-1949 or business@simonandschuster.com.
The Simon & Schuster Speakers Bureau can bring authors to your live event.
For more information or to book an event, contact the Simon & Schuster Speakers Bureau at
1-866-248-3049 or visit our website at www.simonspeakers.com.
Book design by Sonia Chaghatzbanian
The text for this book is set in Eatwell Chubby.
The illustrations for this book are rendered in watercolor.
Manufactured in China
0212 SCP
First Edition
2 4 6 8 10 9 7 5 3 1
Library of Congress Cataloging-in-Publication Data
Fox, Mem, 1946–
Two little monkeys / Mem Fox ; illustrated by Jill Barton.—1st ed.
p. cm.
Summary: A rhyming tale about two little monkeys who are hiding from a leopard.
ISBN 978-1-4169-8687-4 (hardcover)
ISBN 978-1-4424-3577-3 (eBook)
[1. Stories in rhyme. 2. Monkeys—Fiction. 3. Leopard—Fiction.] I. Barton, Jill, ill. II. Title.
PZ8.3.F8245Tw 2010
[E]—dc22
2009021995